**Praise for**

# TIME SPIES

"What a fun adventure! And a fascinating journey through history at the same time!"
—*Marion Dane Bauer, author of the Newbery-Honor winning book,* On My Honor

"The energetic storyline and humor will keep kids reading . . ."
—*Joan Holub, author of the* Doll Hospital *series*

"Kids will hardly realize how much they're learning while caught up in the fun, intrigue and pleasure of these stories."
—*Sally Keehn, author of* Gnat Stokes and the Foggy Bottom Swamp Queen

# TIME SPIES

# TIME SPIES

## Bones in the Badlands
### A Tale of American Dinosaurs

**By Candice Ransom**
**Illustrated by Greg Call**

**MIRRORSTONE**

Cover and interior art by Greg Call
First Printing: October 2006
Library of Congress Catalog Card Number: 2005935558

9 8 7 6 5 4 3

ISBN-10: 0-7869-4028-X
ISBN-13: 978-0-7869-4028-8
620-95556740-001-EN

U.S., CANADA,                                       EUROPEAN HEADQUARTERS
ASIA, PACIFIC, & LATIN AMERICA                      Hasbro UK Ltd
Wizards of the Coast, Inc.                          Caswell Way
P.O. Box 707                                        Newport, Gwent NP9 0YH
Renton, WA 98057-0707                               Great Britain
+1-800-324-6496                                     Please keep this address for your records

Visit our Web site at **www.mirrorstonebooks.com**

To Ben, who is a great reader

# Contents

# The Famous Neighbor

Mattie peered into the dining room. The guests—an older man, a young couple, and a red-haired woman—were finishing breakfast.

"What are you doing?" asked Mattie's brother, Alex.

"Just checking," she said.

"Nobody stayed in the Jefferson Suite last night," he reminded her. "That's the only room the Travel Guide sleeps in."

"I know," Mattie said.

Alex slumped against the doorframe. "It's been two weeks since our last adventure. I'm beginning to think we'll never get to use the spyglass again."

"Maybe that won't be so bad," said Mattie.

He looked at her. "But the spyglass is the only exciting thing about this old place."

"Guess what?" Five-year-old Sophie skipped in, carrying her stuffed elephant, Ellsworth, as always. "Daddy's taking us someplace today!"

Since the Chapman family had moved to Virginia a few weeks ago, their parents had been busy running the Gray Horse Inn. Except for a secret journey back in time to the Revolutionary War, the kids hadn't been anywhere.

"I'd love to go to the movies," said Mattie. "Or shopping!"

"I'd rather go to a water park," Alex said.

But their father had another idea.

"We're going to Monticello," Mr. Chapman announced as they piled into the minivan.

Mattie frowned. "Monticello? Isn't that Thomas Jefferson's house?"

Alex rolled his eyes at Mattie. "Another old house."

"I know," she groaned. "I thought we were going to have *fun* today."

She and Alex sat in silence as they rode down the highway. Soon Mr. Chapman pulled into an enormous parking lot that was already nearly full. They got out of the car and joined a line to buy tickets. When it was Mr. Chapman's turn, the woman in the booth stared at Mattie.

"Is she over eleven?" the woman asked.

Mattie tossed her hair and smiled.

"No," Alex answered. "She's only nine."

"Nine and a *half*," Mattie said, "which is a lot older than just barely eight."

"I've been eight for two whole months—"

Mr. Chapman held up a hand. "Please. We came here to have fun."

Mattie and Alex exchanged dark looks as they stood in yet another line. In a few minutes, a small white bus scooted up.

The bus dropped them off by the biggest brick house Mattie had ever seen. Four massive pillars held up the porch roof. The second story of the house was capped with a white dome that shone in the sun.

The guide led them up the porch steps and opened the huge front door.

Mr. Chapman held Sophie's hand as they entered the house. Mattie and Alex followed, their footsteps echoing in the enormous hall.

"In Mr. Jefferson's time," the guide said in

her ringing voice, "the entrance hall was a waiting room for visitors. It also served as a kind of museum."

Mattie tuned out the guide's speech. She wasn't interested in marble busts or old deer antlers. How *boring*, she thought, yawning.

The group shuffled into another part of the house. In Jefferson's office, Alex nudged Mattie. "Look at that!"

A telescope stood on a brass three-legged stand in the windowsill. Its wood and brass case gleamed like gold.

"It's just like ours!" Alex whispered.

Mattie looked at the spyglass more closely. It *was* identical to their spyglass at home. She wondered if Jefferson's spyglass was magical too.

She tried to move closer but her father

said, "Come on. We're falling behind."

As they moved from room to room, the guide told them about Thomas Jefferson's life. He wrote the Declaration of Independence and was the third president of the United States.

"Jefferson did not like too many servants around," the guide explained, as they entered the dining room. She pushed on the edge of a door. It pivoted inward, revealing shelves built on the other side.

"Instead of bringing food from the kitchen, a servant would set plates on these shelves and turn the door." She spun the door again. "That way Jefferson and his guests wouldn't be disturbed."

Mattie elbowed Alex. "The door turns the same way the bookcase door does in our tower room!"

When the kids first moved to Gray Horse

Inn, they wondered how to get into the third-floor room of the stone tower. There were no doors, only a small bookcase against the wall. Eventually they discovered that the bookcase was really the entrance.

"Do you think Thomas Jefferson built the bookcase door in our house?" Alex asked.

Mattie frowned. "I'm not sure. But it is weird that we have the same stuff in our house that Jefferson did." She stared at the door. "It can't be a coincidence."

The tour ended in the entrance hall. Mattie and Alex wandered around the huge room. Sophie's sandals pattered on the painted green floor.

"I'm pooped," Alex complained. "I want to sit down."

"You can't sit on the chairs," Sophie said, twirling Ellsworth. "They're *an-teeks*."

Mattie gazed at a strange, dark gray object on a nearby table. It was a half circle with a triangle-shaped point sticking out the top. Mattie thought it looked like the model of the human jaw at their dentist's office.

"Alex," she said. "Look."

Alex came over. "Cool! A fossil!"

Mattie read the little card, " 'Jawbone of a Mastodon.' Isn't a mastodon some kind of ancient elephant? Its tooth is bigger than my hand!"

"If Jefferson collected neat stuff like this, he couldn't be all bad," Alex said.

Sophie quit twirling and said, "Tomorrow."

"What about tomorrow?" asked Mattie.

But Sophie had run across the room to grab her father's hand.

# The New Travel Guide

The smell of warm chocolate tickled Mattie's nose. Her father's chocolate-chip muffins. He baked them every Tuesday morning.

Morning! Mattie's eyes flew open. She threw the covers back and dressed quickly in shorts and a T-shirt. In the hall, she collided with Alex.

"The Travel Guide is here!" he cried.

"How do you know?"

"Mom said a guest came late last night," he said. "She asked to stay in the Jefferson Suite!"

"Oh, Alex, I'm so nervous! Where do you think we'll go?"

"I hope we go to the rain forest," Alex said.

Sophie came out of her bedroom, carrying Ellsworth. "We're hungry," she said. Winchester, who was more Sophie's cat than anyone's, followed her.

"Eat a big breakfast," Mattie told them. "If we have another adventure today, who knows when we'll eat again!"

Mattie's stomach fluttered with butterflies when she entered the dining room.

She recognized the guests seated at one end of the long table. The couple, the red-haired woman, and the older man talked and laughed as they ate.

Then she saw a tan woman with dark brown hair and rimless glasses at the other end of the table. She sipped coffee as she skimmed the newspaper headlines. When she heard the kids come in, she looked up and smiled.

"Good morning," she said. "You must be— wait, I think I have it." She pointed to them each in turn. "Mattie . . . Sophie . . . and of course you're Alex."

Mattie let out the breath she had been holding. The new Travel Guide must be a wizard!

"How did you know who we are?" Alex asked.

The woman laughed. "Your mother showed me your pictures. We sat up chatting until after midnight." She waved at three empty chairs. "Please sit down. I'm Ms. Van Hoven."

Mattie took the chair closest to Ms. Van

11

Hoven. Would she give them a signal that she was definitely their next Travel Guide?

The first Travel Guide, a man named Mr. Jones, had greeted them wearing the uniform of a soldier in General George Washington's army. Mr. Jones was a reenactor, playing the part of a real soldier in a staged Revolutionary War battle.

The kids thought Mr. Jones was a bit strange, and when they realized he had started them on adventures back in time, they knew his visit was no accident.

But Ms. Van Hoven looked perfectly normal in khaki shorts and a navy polo shirt. When Mattie noticed the woman's hiking boots and thick socks, she asked, "Did you climb our mountain this morning?"

The Chapmans owned seventy acres of Wildcat Mountain, which rose steeply behind their house. A winding trail led to the top.

Ms. Van Hoven laughed. "I strolled around your garden this morning, but that was it. I'm wearing hiking boots because they are part of my work uniform."

Alex was heaping his plate with two ham steaks and a bagel. He kicked Mattie under the table and mouthed the word, "Uniform."

Mattie rubbed her shin. She wanted to kick him back, and then realized they had just been given an important clue. Would all Travel Guides wear a uniform to let the kids know their identity?

Buttering a bagel, Alex asked Ms. Van Hoven, "Do you run a bulldozer? I mean, I've seen bulldozer drivers. They wear boots and shorts in hot weather."

"Bones," Sophie said suddenly. She had cut out the round bone from her ham steak and balanced it on the end of her index finger.

Mattie frowned at her. "Soph, you're not supposed to play with your food."

Sophie poked the ham bone through the hole in her bagel. "No, that's the lady's job. Bones."

Ms. Van Hoven winked at Sophie. "You're right, Sophie. My job is bones."

"Are you a doctor?" Alex asked. He wrinkled his nose at Mattie. Neither of them wanted to go on an adventure that involved hospitals or medicine.

"Yes, but not the kind you're thinking of," Ms. Van Hoven replied. "I'm a scientist. A paleontologist, to be exact. I dig up fossils and study them."

Alex dropped his bagel. "You dig up dinosaurs?"

Ms. Van Hoven nodded. "I'm on my way to

the University of Virginia. There's an exhibition and lecture on Ice Age fossils."

"Those aren't dinosaurs," Mattie said.

"No, the dinosaurs came earlier. The animals that followed were woolly mammoths, saber-toothed tigers, sloths, mastodons—"

"Mastodons," Mattie repeated. "We saw a mastodon jawbone just yesterday. In Thomas Jefferson's house."

Ms. Van Hoven reached for the muffin basket. "Thomas Jefferson was very interested in mastodons. He asked William Clark, an explorer, to find mastodon fossils. Clark went to the Ohio Valley and sent back teeth, jawbones, a tusk, and other fossils. Jefferson displayed some of the bones in the front hall of Monticello."

"We saw all kinds of neat stuff at Jefferson's house yesterday," Mattie said. "He invented a machine that made copies of letters and a clock that told the day of the week—"

"And a spyglass," Alex blurted.

Now Mattie kicked *him* under the table. They weren't supposed to talk about the tower or the spyglass, especially with other people around.

Ms. Van Hoven didn't seem to notice.

"Jefferson wrote about prehistoric Virginia," she said. "Or as much as people knew in the seventeen hundreds."

Mattie had a scary thought. Suppose they went back to prehistoric Virginia!

"Do you hunt for fossils around here?" Mattie asked Ms. Van Hoven.

Before answering, Ms. Van Hoven got up and took a postcard from a basket on the sideboard. She glanced at the picture on the front, a photograph of the Gray Horse

Inn, then turned the postcard over and began writing in the message space.

"I wish I worked in a place as beautiful as the Blue Ridge mountains," she said, as she scribbled. "No, I'm on a dig in the Badlands."

"How can land be bad?" Alex asked.

"In some parts out west, like South Dakota, Wyoming, and Nebraska, the land is very rough. Lots of steep rocks and canyons," said Ms. Van Hoven. "The Lakota tribe called the area *mako sica*, which means 'bad lands.' It is very hot and dry there. Some days it's over a hundred and ten degrees."

"Is your job dangerous?" asked Mattie.

"We have to do a lot of climbing. And watch out for rattlesnakes. I found one in my sleeping bag once. Luckily it didn't bite me."

Mattie gazed at the woman. Maybe *she'd* be a paleontologist when she grew up. But only if she could work where there weren't any snakes.

"How come you're here?" Alex asked.

"I'm on vacation and I came east to visit friends and see this exhibition." Ms. Van Hoven checked her wristwatch. "Which reminds me. I'd better get moving. The lecture starts in less than an hour. Please excuse me."

She got up again, nodding to the other guests. Then she dropped the postcard in the silver tray marked *Outgoing Mail* and went upstairs.

Mattie was bursting with curiosity. The postcard was actually the ticket to their next adventure. But she couldn't look at it until everyone had left the dining room.

Mattie hopped up and began clearing plates and glasses. "You're done, aren't you?" she said to the older man, tugging the coffee cup out of his hand.

Mrs. Chapman came in just then. "Mattie! Let Mr. Riley finish his coffee."

"He looked done," Mattie fibbed, trailing her mother into the kitchen with a load of dirty dishes.

Alex bumped through the swinging door with the platters of ham and scrambled eggs. Sophie followed with the bagel and muffin baskets.

At last, the guests wandered off. When the dining room was finally empty, Mattie pounced on the postcard in the tray.

She read the note Ms. Van Hoven had written.

Need a field assistant. Where is Pete?
—W.G.

"It doesn't make sense," said Alex.

"The last postcard didn't make sense either, until we came back home and figured it out."

Alex jostled her elbow. "What's the picture?"

Mattie covered the postcard with her left hand. "I'm scared to look! She talked about dinosaurs and saber-toothed tigers. What if we land in the middle of a dinosaur fight or something?"

"Turn it over!"

Mattie flipped the postcard. Instead of the photograph of the Gray Horse Inn, the scene showed a barren, moonlike landscape in faded shades of brown. There were no people in the picture, only some sort of structure along a ridge.

"What *is* that?" she said.

"It doesn't look very exciting," Alex said, sounding disappointed. "Our other postcard was the Battle of Yorktown."

"Nothing but rocks," she said, though she was glad not to see a couple of snarling T. rexes.

Sophie stood on tiptoe to see the postcard. "Oh, boy!"

"What do you know that we don't?" Mattie asked her.

"C'mon!" She pulled Mattie and Alex toward the staircase.

They climbed the steps to the second floor and then up the steeper stairs to the third floor. The Jefferson Suite occupied one end of the third floor. Its door stood open and the kids could see the neatly made bed. No sign of Ms. Van Hoven. It was as if she had never stayed overnight.

Opposite the Jefferson Suite, a small bookcase was built into an otherwise blank wall. Alex pushed the edge of the bookcase and the shelves swiveled partway into a room.

The kids crawled through the opening on their hands and knees. They stood up in the windowed tower room. Mattie carefully closed the door so their entrance would remain hidden.

Alex ran over to the only piece of furniture

in the room, a desk. He opened a secret panel on one side and took out a box. Inside the box was a polished brass and wood tube. Alex extended the tube until the sections stretched into a spyglass.

He gripped the spyglass around the middle. "Ready?"

Mattie glanced at down at her sneakers. Should she change her shoes? They were all wearing shorts, T-shirts, and sneakers. What if they went someplace cold? Or where they looked weird, like they did in the Revolutionary War?

"Mattie!" Alex said. "Hurry up."

Mattie took one end of the spyglass while Sophie touched the other. Half moons, stars, and other strange markings appeared on the wooden case.

The spyglass grew warm beneath Mattie's

hand. Her fingers tingled and she closed her eyes. She felt the floor disappear as if she were falling through a trapdoor.

This part of the magic never failed to frighten her. Down and down she tumbled. Colors swirled around her in dizzying patterns. She could not see Alex or Sophie and hoped they were with her.

At last her feet hit something solid . . . and gritty.

— 3 —

# Cabin of Bones

A hot, dry breeze blew sand into Mattie's eyes. The air felt like a furnace. She squinted in the glaring sunlight. From the position of the sun, she figured it was late afternoon.

"Water!" said Alex, his tongue hanging out dramatically. "I'm dying of thirst!"

"We haven't been here five seconds," Mattie said. She looked around quickly for Sophie. Her little sister stood behind her, clutching Ellsworth.

"I'm hot," said Sophie. "Can we go to the pool?"

Mattie scanned the horizon. Grayish rocks and a few stubby plants stood out against endless sand. The land sloped upward to form a ridge. At the top, she saw the hut shown in the postcard. Across the desert, she noticed a bumpy sheer-faced mountain.

"This sure isn't the rain forest," Alex said, slipping the spyglass in the pocket of his shorts. "There's nobody around here but us. And I *am* dying of thirst."

"Maybe somebody's living in that hut thing," Mattie pointed to the stone structure on top of the ridge. "They'll have water. Let's go up and see."

They started climbing the ridge. Hot stones burned through the soles of Mattie's tennis shoes. She was glad she hadn't worn flip-flops.

Alex puffed along beside her, grinding pebbles beneath his shoes. "If there's nobody up here—" he began.

"Let's not worry about that now," said Mattie.

Normally full of energy, Sophie lagged behind them. Mattie went back and took her sister's sweaty hand.

"It's too hot out here," Sophie whined.

"Ellsworth doesn't mind the heat," Mattie told her. "Her relatives live in Africa. It's hotter than this in Africa. That's why elephants have such thick, tough hides."

"We're not elephants," Alex said.

"Someone will help us," Mattie said. "They'll have cool water and we can rest in the shade."

But when the kids finally reached the top of the ridge, they stopped and stared. The hut was just a pile of stones! Only one wall, the wall they had seen from the bottom of the ridge, was standing. Huge boulders squatted like gigantic toads. The dry, sandy wind kicked up again. No sign of life stirred in the bleak landscape.

"Now what?" Alex said.

"I really thought somebody would be up here," Mattie said faintly. What would they do now?

"Should we go back?" Alex started to pull the spyglass from his pocket.

"We don't know what our mission is," Mattie said.

Alex's face was red from the heat. "Maybe the spyglass made a mistake and landed us miles from where we're supposed to be."

"The spyglass doesn't make mistakes," Sophie said.

"Yeah," said Mattie. "This place looks just like it did in the postcard."

"What if we go home and get some water?" Alex asked. "I think we need stuff for this mission. Water bottles, sunscreen—"

"Sunhats," Mattie murmured. "That's what I was wondering before we fell through time. If we were wearing the right clothes."

"So we're going back?"

She hesitated. "I don't know if we should. On our first trip, we left before we figured out why we were there."

"Thomas Jefferson and Captain Jack were after us!" Alex said. "It didn't hurt anything when we left."

Mattie sat down on an oblong boulder. She couldn't think in this heat. The rock was scooped in the middle, like a seat. Her index finger traced circles on its rough surface.

*Maybe Alex is right*, she thought. Maybe they should grab the spyglass and go back home for supplies. But if they came prepared, it could mess up the magic somehow.

Like they were *expecting* what they had to do. They were supposed to learn their mission after they got to their destination.

Her fingernail snagged on a chip in the boulder. She chewed the jagged nail, staring at the rock. The light gray surface was etched with large, darker gray circles.

She stood up to see the rock better. It reminded her of something . . .

Last summer she had made friendship bracelets. If she enlarged one of the beads a thousand times, it would look like this boulder. But what kind of a rock looked like a giant plastic bead?

"Holy smokes," Alex cried. "Do you know what you've been sitting on?"

She jumped away as if she'd been stung. "No, what?"

"A *bone*!"

"What?" She viewed the boulder from another angle. "It *is*! What kind of animal has bones that big?"

"Only one, Matt." Alex's eyes were shining. "A dinosaur!"

She gaped at him. "You're kidding!"

"Really. I think this is a part of a dinosaur's backbone. It looks like a model we had in school. Only way bigger."

He bounded from boulder to boulder. "Bone!" he said, slapping a long rock lying on its side. "Another bone! Mattie, they're *all* bones!"

Her head spun. What kind of a place *was* this? Then she noticed Sophie climbing on the ruins of the hut.

"Soph, be careful!" She scurried over.

Sophie "walked" Ellsworth along the top of a craggy rock. "Ellsworth is a scientist back in the olden days," she said.

"Who would ever be a scientist here?" Mattie said, helping Sophie safely down from the rubble. Then she stared at the base of the wall.

All the rocks were bones! Big bones, little bones. Broken bones. Bone chips and fragments. The entire hut had been built from bones!

"Alex!" she shrieked.

He ran over. "Cool! Somebody made a house out of dinosaur bones! I wish it were still standing. Wouldn't it be neat to live here?"

"It wouldn't be very comfortable," Mattie said.

"I bet we can find a whole dinosaur if we just—"

Sophie interrupted, "Somebody's coming."

Mattie heard small scuffing sounds, like boots kicking pebbles.

"She's right," she said. "We'd better hide!"

"There!" Alex pointed to a long rock. They dashed over and ducked behind it.

"Guess what?" Alex whispered.

"What?" Mattie whispered back.

Alex ran his hand over the boulder. "This is really a leg bone, not a rock!"

Mattie poked him. Then she peeked over the crest of the leg bone.

A tall, rangy man strode toward the ruins. He wore cowboy boots, grimy jeans, and a shirt with the sleeves rolled above his elbows. He was so tan his skin was like leather.

Propping one dusty boot on a boulder, the man unhooked a canteen from his belt. He tipped his head back and drank deeply.

"He's got water!" Sophie cried.

"Shhh!" Mattie hissed. "We don't know him."

"He's the scientist man," Sophie insisted. "He's nice! He'll give us water."

Before Mattie could stop her, Sophie ran out from behind the leg bone.

"Soph, no!" Mattie cried.

— 4 —

# Dinosaur Cowboys

The stranger jerked his arm, spilling the canteen. "What on earth—?"

Sophie went right up to him. "Can I have some water? Please?"

The man smiled in relief, as if he'd finally realized Sophie was only a little girl. "Of course, young lady." He gave her the canteen.

Drawn by the sight of water, Mattie and Alex hurried over too.

"No need to stampede," the man said. "Plenty for all."

When it was her turn, Mattie tilted the brass canteen and began to drink. The water wasn't cold, but nothing had ever tasted so wonderful. She wiped her mouth with the back of her hand and passed the canteen to Alex.

"Why are you children out here with no water?" the man asked. "How did you get up this bluff? Where are your folks?"

Glancing at Alex, Mattie decided to play dumb.

"We don't know how we got up here," she said slowly.

"You don't know?" the man repeated in disbelief. "Did you sprout wings and fly?"

"My sister means . . . ," Alex said, "she means we're lost. We don't know where we are."

The man took off his hat and scratched his head. Mattie noticed his ears stuck out. She wanted to giggle but figured this was not a good time.

"You must be addled from the sun," he said to them. "Come on. Let's get out of the heat."

He set off down the ridge, his long legs gobbling up ground. Mattie and the others rushed to catch up with him.

"Sir!" she said. "What's your name?"

"Walter Granger," he replied. "What's yours?"

"Mattie Chapman," she said. "This is my brother, Alex, and my sister, Sophie."

"And *this* is Ellsworth." Sophie wiggled her stuffed animal.

Mattie wondered if Mr. Granger was the person they were supposed to meet. That was the problem with going back in time. The postcard showed them where they were going, but didn't tell them their mission. The kids had to make excuses about why they were there until they could figure it out.

At the bottom of the ridge, Mr. Granger headed toward a large rocky outcropping. The land sloped downward like a basin.

On the other side of the rock formation, four white canvas tents poked up like miniature mountains. Each tent was held up in the middle by a single pole.

A wagon packed with boxes stood under the feeble shade of a scrawny tree. Just beyond, several horses grazed on scrubby grass. They were each tied to a stake driven into the ground. Mattie figured that kept them from running off.

Three men milled around a camp stove ringed with wooden boxes. When the men saw the kids, they gawked.

A slim man marched forward, carrying a tin coffeepot.

"Glory be!" he cried. "Where'd you find young'uns way out here, Walt?"

"They were hiding behind the femur of a giant saurian," said Mr. Granger. "Popped up like prairie dogs. Nearly scared the wits out of me."

"Wish I could have seen that." The man grinned through his brushy beard. "I'm Jacob Wortman. Hungry? We're fixing a bite to eat."

Walter Granger led them to the campsite. "Have a seat. Sam O'Malley will fetch you more water. Drink slowly," he cautioned the kids. "You don't want a bellyache." He disappeared into one of the tents.

"Hi," said a young blond man. He gave them each a tin mug of water. "I'm Sam. Supper will be ready in a minute."

Mattie sipped her water and looked around. An upended box to her left served as a desk. Its surface was cluttered with papers and maps. A weather-beaten leather journal lay open, weighted with stones so the wind wouldn't blow it away.

The pages were covered with numbers and messy handwriting. Mattie made out one word—B*rontosaurus*. It had been underlined twice. A brontosaurus was a giant dinosaur, she knew.

Just then Walter Granger returned with a paper that said *The Western Union Telegraph Company* at the top. He slipped a corner of the paper under one of the stones on his desk.

"Help yourself to some stew," he said to the kids. "Norman and Sam haven't set up the chow tent yet. The food might improve a *little* when they do." The corners of his eyes crinkled with laughter.

"You won't find better grub east of the Missouri River," said the sandy-haired man bent over the camp stove.

"We'd find better food east of Como Station," Sam joked, handing Mattie a stack of tin plates and some spoons. "Norman Grant here only knows how to fix two things. Beans and sheep stew!"

Mattie gulped. *Sheep* stew?

"You'll be glad enough for my cooking after you've been digging all day," Norman shot back.

Mattie leaned over the smoky camp stove. *Please*, she thought. *Let it be beans today.* But when she dipped the ladle into the pot, she saw chunks of grayish meat floating in a scummy gravy.

41

"It's sheep stew," she said in a low tone to Alex.

Alex smacked his lips as if they were having pizza and ice cream. "Give me a lot. I want to eat like a real Wild West cowboy!" He took his plate and sat with the men.

Mattie spooned a small amount of stew on Sophie's plate and an even tinier amount on her own. Mattie pushed her food around, hoping nobody would notice she wasn't eating.

"It's not your mother's fried chicken, is it?" Walter joked. Then his tone became serious. "Where are you kids from?"

Questions were tricky. Mattie had to answer carefully. "Virginia," she said.

His eyebrows lifted. "Way back east? Where are your parents?"

"Far away, in the country. They sent us to live with our aunt but we got separated from her—" She glanced at the wagon. "On the wagon train."

"Wagon train?" Walter frowned. "In 1898? Why not take the train? The Union Pacific stops at Como Station, just a few miles away."

Mattie flicked a glance at Alex. Now they knew the year they had gone back to. And the place, sort of. But she needed to fix her mistake.

"Well, it wasn't *exactly* a wagon train," she said. "It was just one wagon."

"Where was your aunt taking you?" Walter asked.

"Her house," Alex put in. "But we don't know where it is. We've never been to—" His arm swept out, indicating the land around them.

"Wyoming," Walter supplied.

"Yeah," Alex said. "We've never been to Wyoming before."

Walter stared at their shorts. "Judging from the ragged state of your pants, it's obvious you've been on your own some time now."

"We've done okay," Mattie said. She couldn't tell him they were actually wearing almost new clothes.

Walter nodded, as if he had come to a decision. "Tomorrow I'll ride to Como Station and telegraph a friend. A nurse in Laramie. I'll ask her to take you to the orphanage in Laramie until your parents—or your aunt—can be found."

Mattie's heart skipped. "How long will that take?"

"A week."

She let out her breath. A whole week should be plenty of time to finish their mission, whatever it was.

Norman and Sam started unloading lumber

from the wagon. Jacob pounded a pole into the ground. "For your tent," Jacob explained.

"It's cooling off," Walter said. "Why don't we take a walk while the men here finish up your tent."

They headed away from the camp, down what seemed to be a dried-up streambed. Rocks of every shape and size littered the surface. The jagged bluff soared above them. On the other side, the ridge with the hut at the top rose like stair steps.

"How come you're camping here?" Alex asked.

"I head a group of fossil collectors," Walter explained. "I work for a man named Professor Osborn at the American Museum of Natural History in New York City. Our team digs up dinosaur bones and sends them back to the museum." Walter chuckled. "People sometimes call us dinosaur cowboys because we hunt for dinosaur bones."

"We've never been to New York," Alex said. "But once we went to the Smithsonian in Washington, D.C. We saw the Hope Diamond and a whale skull hanging from the ceiling—"

Walter stared at him. "I didn't realize the Smithsonian Institute had acquired such wonders."

Mattie elbowed her brother. Clearly Alex had mentioned something that hadn't happened yet in 1898.

"What happens to the bones after they go to New York?" she asked.

"They're cleaned and the skeletons are assembled," Walter replied. "Often bones are missing, so plaster copies are made."

"You have the best job in the world!" Alex said.

Walter smiled. "It doesn't seem like the best job when we have a blinding windstorm. Or when it's a hundred and ten degrees in the shade."

He nudged a large, half-buried rock with the toe of his boot. "We haven't begun to dig yet, but I believe Bone Cabin Quarry will prove to be a rich source of fossils."

"What's a quarrel?" Sophie asked.

"A quarry," Walter corrected. "That means a place where you dig out special rocks, or in this case, fossilized bones. I named this place Bone Cabin Quarry after the ruins of that cabin on the hill where I found you."

"Who would build a cabin out of dinosaur bones?" Mattie asked.

"Few people can tell rocks from fossils. The sheepherders who built the cabin had no idea."

Alex picked up a small rock. "Is this a fossil?"

Walter nodded. "That's part of a jawbone, maybe from a crocodile."

"Crocodile!" Alex sounded doubtful. "In the desert?"

"This land wasn't always desert."

"It was the ocean." Sophie sat in the dirt, piling stones.

Walter looked down at her in surprise. "How could you possibly know that?"

Alex changed the subject quickly. "Can we help you find bones? We're good at messing around in the dirt."

"Working with fossils is more complicated than you think," he said. "But you might be able to do simple fieldwork."

"What about me and Sophie?" Mattie asked eagerly.

Walter shook his head. "This work is too hard for girls."

"I'm just as strong as Alex!" she protested. "Plus I'm a whole year older."

"Sorry," he told her. "The field can be dangerous—rattlesnakes, rockslides, storms, heat—"

Mattie's temper flared. "That's not fair! Anyway, girls have smaller fingers. Sophie and I would be way better at cleaning bones."

Walter nodded thoughtfully. "It's true . . . Inexperienced fieldworkers often pick up a fossil, only to have it crumble like a biscuit. Sometimes men's fingers *are* too clumsy."

"Then can we help?"

He gave in. "You can be my assistant. But you must also watch your little sister."

The sun had slid behind the bluff, highlighting bands of colors in the rocks. Pale gray, dark brown, pink, purple, pale yellow, gray-green.

"Those stripes show the different prehistoric eras—Jurassic, Triassic, and Cretaceous. You can read the history of this place like a book! Look at this!" Walter pointed to a pair of huge birdlike footprints.

"Dinosaur tracks!" Alex breathed.

"I'll make a cast of them in the morning," said Walter.

They headed back to camp. Bones stuck out of the wall of the bluff and up from the floor of the basin. The kids were in awe.

Walter Granger touched a rib bone as tall as he was and ran his hands along the wide plate of a giant shoulder blade.

"We have a treasure trove here," he murmured. "But we must be careful. Other people would like to take these fossils from us. We can't let that happen."

"How would they know where to find the fossils?" asked Mattie.

"By spying on us." Walter stared warily at the ridge for a moment and then he cleared his throat. "Better turn in soon. Tomorrow will be a busy day."

Inside their tent, the kids settled in their bed-rolls. Sophie dropped off almost instantly, Ellsworth tucked in the crook of her arm.

Mattie leaned on one elbow. "You heard what Walter said about people spying."

"Yeah," said Alex. "You don't think he meant us?"

"No, but I bet that's our mission. We were sent here to keep spies away. These guys are going to do important work. Maybe discover a brand-new dinosaur."

"We're going to be here at least a week," he

said. "That's when Walter's friend is supposed to take us to the orphanage. We've never been gone this long. Do you think Mom and Dad will miss us?"

"Last time it was like we'd only been gone a few minutes," Mattie replied. She hoped this would be a short mission, especially if they had to eat sheep stew.

Alex pulled his blanket up. "Hey, Matt, did you ever think you'd be a dinosaur cowboy?"

"Never in a million years." Then she fell asleep too.

# The Bone Wars

"For your first job as my assistant," Walter told Mattie, "coat this ring with grease." He handed her a large tin ring and a can of sheep fat.

Wincing, Mattie stuck her fingers in the goopy grease and spread it around the inside of the ring.

Walter laid the ring over the dinosaur tracks so they were inside the circle. Then he poured a creamy mixture of plaster over the prints.

"We'll let that dry," he said. They walked over to the dig site.

Alex and the men had used picks and shovels to break large chunks of rocks away from the dinosaur shoulder bone. More of the bone could be seen, though it still wore a shell of stone.

The diggers stopped for a water break. Alex gulped from the canteen, then poured the rest on his head.

"I've never been so hot in my life!" He walked up to Mattie with water dripping down his face.

Mattie glanced at the thermometer hanging from a nail on the wagon. "What do you expect? It's a hundred and thirteen degrees!"

Sophie was building a rock tower. "Your nose is peeling," she said to Alex.

"They didn't have sunscreen in 1898!" He showed them the red marks on his palms. "That's from the shovel. What's so great about this job, I'd like to know."

"Yesterday you said it was the best job in the world," Mattie reminded him.

"Easy for you to say. You hardly do anything." His stomach growled. "I hope we don't have beans for lunch. We had them for breakfast."

"I thought you liked living like a cowboy."

"Just for that," Alex whispered to Mattie, "I'm going to tell Norman how much you love his sheep stew! I'll tell him to fix it every day."

"Don't you dare!" Mattie said.

Walter jumped down into the pit.

"Ladies and gentlemen," he called out with rising excitement. "We have found a stegosaurus!"

The kids ran over to the dig.

"Wow!" Alex breathed. "Isn't that the dinosaur with the plates along its back?"

"How did you know that?" Walter asked in astonishment.

"We saw a model of one at the Smithsonian," Alex replied. "They call it Old

Moneybags because it's supposed to be stuffed with hundred dollar bills!"

Walter gave Alex a peculiar look. "I'm beginning to think you children are paleontologists in disguise."

"Us?" Mattie laughed falsely. Then she asked, "How can you tell there's more of the dinosaur down here? Looks like plain old rock to me."

Walter tipped his hat back. "Most living things decay when they die. But sometimes they become preserved."

Sophie toppled her rock tower and said, "Then they're fossils."

"That's right. Fossils are made when a dead creature is covered quickly with sand or mud. Then it can't be disturbed for a long time. The mud seeps into the bones of the creature and turns them to stone. This takes millions of years."

"So all these bones are millions of years old?" Mattie was impressed.

He nodded. "Now, let's get to work before we become fossils ourselves!"

At lunchtime, Mattie was relieved to see leftover breakfast beans in the stew pot instead of boiled sheep.

Walter scraped the last of the beans from his tin plate. "Sam and I are going to Como Station to pick up supplies. I'll telegraph Lavinia Perkins while I'm there. You kids want to come along?"

"Yeah!" they chorused.

Walter and Sam rode their own horses, and each led a packhorse. Alex straddled behind Walter on his brown horse. Sophie sat in front of Sam on his black horse. They followed the railroad tracks to the station, eight miles away. The trip took forever. Mattie bumped along on the back of one of the packhorses. She wished they had a car.

Como Station consisted of a couple of shacks right next to the tracks and a water tower that looked like an old-fashioned coffeepot.

"The supplies are in there," Walter told Sam, indicating the second building. "I'm going to the stationmaster's office to send the telegram."

"You kids help me load up," Sam told them.

They hauled sacks of coffee, beans, salt, and other food to the packhorses.

"Good, my apples are here," Sam said, strapping the sack of apples with other parcels of food. He hoisted four kegs of water, four rolls of burlap, and two sacks of plaster of paris across the horses' backs.

"What do you need the burlap and the plaster for?" asked Alex.

"We wrap the bones in burlap soaked in plaster," Sam replied. "To protect them when they're shipped to the museum."

Next they went into the stationmaster's office.

A small man wearing round wire-rimmed eyeglasses was tapping on an odd device. His bald head had exactly four strands of hair combed over it. Mattie counted them. She moved closer to see the device better.

The small brass platform had a brass "arm" with a flat-topped wooden knob on one end. The man tapped the wooden knob, which made clicking sounds.

She looked around the cluttered office. Papers were scattered on the desk. Old newspapers lay heaped in the corners. A row of bright red apples on the windowsill lent the only cheery note.

The man clicked the device a few more times then stopped. "That's it. Twenty-five cents, please."

Walter paid him. "I'll come back day after tomorrow for my reply, Otto."

"Fine." Otto waved a limp hand.

Mattie's heart sped up. They could be on their way to the orphanage in Laramie even sooner than a week! That didn't leave much time to accomplish their mission. They hadn't even seen anything suspicious yet.

"What's that thing?" Sophie asked Otto, pointing to the clicking device.

"A telegraph key," he replied. "I send messages over the telegraph wires along the train tracks. Each click you hear is part of a code. I also receive messages in the same code."

"Better be careful what you write in a telegram," Walter said jokingly. "Otto reads them all."

"We didn't get all our supplies," Sam told Walter. "Only half the burlap and plaster came in."

"The rest is on another train," said Otto. "Should be here day after tomorrow." He fished something out of the paper pile. "This telegram came in earlier."

"Thanks." Walter put the envelope in his shirt pocket.

By the time they arrived back at camp, it was evening. After supper, everyone relaxed around the stove.

Walter pulled the paper Otto had given

him from his pocket. As he shook the envelope, a gust of wind tore across the campsite,
sending the telegram flying.

Mattie jumped up and trapped the paper
against a tumbleweed.

Handwritten words leaped out at her:

"Thanks." Walter took the paper and they sat down again.

Jacob whittled a stick with his jackknife. "I remember when you couldn't spit without hitting somebody out here. There were more fossil hunters than buffalo! Especially during the height of the Bone Wars."

"Bone Wars?" Mattie echoed. She hoped they hadn't landed in the middle of another war!

"It wasn't a real war," Walter explained. "More like a feud. Two scientists from different museums tried to see who could find the most species of dinosaurs."

"Who won?" Alex wanted to know.

"Professor Cope died just last year," replied Walter. "But my guess is that Professor Marsh will claim the title. He discovered dozens of species."

"Are the Bone Wars still going on?" Sophie asked.

"Somewhat. When the feud was at its peak, both teams spied on each other to see who found the best dig sites. Today, there are still expedition teams like ours. They work for other museums or for people who want dinosaur bones. That is why we must guard our secret."

"People will do anything for a dime," Sam said, biting into an apple. "Even sell our dinosaur bones."

# — 6 —

# The Dinosaur Graveyard

Mattie sat at a small wooden table and bent over long claws encased in rock. A box of small brushes and tools rested on top of the table. With a sharp metal tool, Mattie scraped dirt from between the dinosaur's fingers.

The team had found another dinosaur. Walter called it "bird-robber." Mattie decided the dinosaur was a girl and gave her a nicer name.

"Olivia," she said to the fossilized hand. "You really need a manicure."

Sophie looked up from her rock village and giggled. "We don't have any nail polish, silly!"

"Olivia won't mind," Mattie said. "So long as we get her claws clean."

Mattie blew away loose particles. She was enjoying her work on the dig so much she had almost forgotten why they were at Bone Cabin Quarry. So far nothing strange had happened. Was it possible the Travel Guide was wrong? Maybe Mr. Granger didn't really need their help.

But if that were true, Mattie decided, the spyglass would not have sent them to Wyoming. She felt certain the spyglass did not make mistakes.

Professor Osborn had warned Walter about poachers. Mattie was pretty sure a poacher was someone who hunts on somebody else's land. In this case, someone who hunts dinosaur bones. She glanced up at the bluff. Poachers could be anywhere. One could be high up in the rocks, watching them right now.

Suddenly there was a shout from the site. Mattie saw Alex thrust his fist to the sky.

"Yes!" he cried.

Mattie dropped her brush and ran to the dig. "What is it?"

Norman grinned up at her. "We've found even more dinosaurs! This place is a dinosaur boneyard!"

"Boneyard?" she echoed. "Is that like a graveyard?"

"Exactly! More dinosaurs than we dreamed! They're piled on top of each other, two, three, even four deep!" Norman did a little jig.

"The one beneath the stegosaurus is a

monster," Alex told Mattie. "It's a—what did you call it?"

"Allosaurus," Jacob replied. "A ferocious meat-eating saurian."

"Our site is more valuable than ever," said Walter. "It won't remain a secret once we start sending bones back to New York. But we must keep our location quiet as long as possible."

"Claims get jumped all the time," Sam said.

"Claims? Like in the gold rush days?" Mattie asked. "Back when people went to California to find gold?"

Sam nodded. "Only instead of claiming a gold mine, somebody could say they found our dig first."

Mattie felt someone tug at her T-shirt. It was Sophie.

"Can I have a brush?" Sophie whispered so no one else could hear. "And one of those pointy metal sticks?"

"What for, Soph?"

"I found a dinosaur."

Mattie smiled. Sophie was so cute! She took her sister back to the table.

"You can borrow a brush and this pick, but don't dare lose them."

"I promise," Sophie said, then skipped back to the other side of the dig.

At lunchtime, Norman Grant surprised them with a new dish.

"Mmmm!" said Alex, cramming a spoonful into his mouth. "What is it?"

"Rabbit," said Norman. "I went hunting before breakfast this morning. What's the matter, Mattie? Don't you like rabbit?"

"Not to *eat*." She pushed her plate away.

Walter frowned. "I thought you children were from the country. Don't you eat live-stock? And the game your father hunts?"

Sweat trickled down Mattie's neck. She thought they were past tricky questions.

"Daddy is a terrible hunter," she said nervously. "And . . . all our cows and pigs are pets."

Sam's blue eyes narrowed. "You must live on a strange farm—" he began.

Before he could finish his sentence, egg-sized drops of rain splattered in the dust.

Walter leaped up. "Cover the dig site! Norm, get the canvas!"

Mattie had never seen rain like this. In an instant she was soaked. Alex hurried to help the men, but Mattie and Sophie ran for their tent.

Just as suddenly as it had begun, the rain stopped and the sun came out. Mattie and Sophie stepped out of the tent and into a muddy mess.

"Yuck," Sophie said. But the sun was so hot, the puddles were already drying up.

At the dig site, Alex and the men were pulling off a huge canvas. Walter ordered Sam to go check the horses. Then he jumped down into the excavation hole.

"Just wet," he reported, crawling out of the hole. "It could have been worse."

"Hey!" bellowed Sam, sprinting toward them. "The horses are gone! Picket pins and all!"

Everyone dashed to the patch of sagebrush and scrub behind the wagon. None of the horses were in sight. Only holes remained where the stakes had been driven into the ground.

Walter scanned the horizon. "Gone is right. Maybe the storm spooked them and they ran off."

"I hammered the pins myself," Sam said. "There's no way the horses could have pulled them loose."

"Then somebody let them go on purpose," Jacob said. His words hung in the hot air.

"Let's look around," said Walter. "Maybe they didn't wander far."

As soon as the men left, Alex said, "Somebody's trying to ruin Walter's dig. Maybe even a spy!"

Mattie nodded. "We have to catch the troublemaker before he does anything worse. Look around for clues."

They located six holes where the stakes had been yanked out of the ground. Mattie got down on her knees.

Among the horseshoe prints stamped in the mud, she saw the faint impressions of many different boots. But where the horses' tracks trailed away from the grazing area, they were accompanied by just one pair of boots.

"Look." She pointed at the set of boot prints. "I bet these were made by the person who let the horses go."

Alex examined them. "They're definitely different than the others. The toe is kind of square." He glanced at Mattie. "Do you think it's one of the men?"

"There's only one way to find out. We'll have to get a boot from each guy and match it."

"Steal one of their boots?" He stared at her. "And how are we going to do that, since they wear them all the time?"

"They don't wear their boots to bed," Mattie said.

Mattie thought the camp would never settle down that night. The men stayed up late, discussing the situation. Finally Walter banked the fire, and they all went into their own tents. When snores mingled with coyote calls, Mattie gave Alex and Sophie the signal to move.

Silently, Mattie slipped her hand into Walter's tent and took one of his boots. Alex collected Sam's and Jacob's boots. Sophie carefully brought back Norman's boot.

"We need light," Mattie whispered, taking three of the boots. She made sure she remembered which boot belonged to which man.

Alex poked a branch into the campfire and lit it to make a torch. "Soph, stay here on guard. If anybody wakes up, pretend you've had a bad dream and make a lot of noise."

"Okay."

It was creepy in the desert at night with only a small torch for light. Mattie and Alex stumbled to the horses' grazing area.

Alex compared his boot to the set of prints. "Jacob's doesn't match."

Mattie checked her boots. "Neither does Norman's. Or Walter's."

Then she placed Sam's boot down to the prints mixed with horse tracks. "Bingo," she said. "These are Sam's prints."

"But why would Sam let the horses go? He takes care of them."

"Wait a minute," Mattie said. "Bring the light closer." She stared closely at the print. "See that diamond mark on the heel? It's not on Sam's boot. Or anybody else's."

The torch sputtered and threatened to go out.

"So these tracks don't match anyone's boots," Alex said. "What does it mean?"

"It could mean Sam has another pair of boots we don't know about," Mattie replied. "Or that somebody else let the horses go."

She shivered in the chilly night air. No doubt about it, someone was trying to ruin the dig.

# — 7 —

# The Headless Monster

"We could make plaster copies of the boot prints," said Mattie, chewing a piece of bacon. "I know how."

The kids sat under the lone tree, eating breakfast. Norman and Sam were out looking for the horses. Walter and Jacob were already working at the dig site.

Alex shook his head. "We don't have time. And I don't know what it would prove. We need more evidence that it's Sam or somebody else. If it's somebody else, who?"

Mattie waved her bacon in the direction of the bluff. "Keep an eye on those rocks. A whole army of spies could hide up there."

The kids filled their canteens and headed for the dig. They found Walter and Jacob in deep conversation.

"What wrong?" Mattie asked.

"The allosaurus skeleton doesn't have a head," said Walter.

Alex's eyes widened. "Wow! What bit his head off?"

"It's not unusual to find skeletons without skulls or with smashed skulls," Walter said. "They are easily crushed. I believe floods washed the skull away."

"Does this mean the dinosaur isn't any good?" Mattie wanted to know.

"The dinosaur would be worth more if we had the skull," Walter said. "It would be a bigger attraction at the museum. But still, even without the head, it's a good find."

Sam and Norman approached the dig site. Sam was finishing an apple and Norman was carrying a sandwich made from the leftover bacon and biscuits.

"Any luck?" Jacob asked.

Sam tossed the apple core aside. "Not even a horseshoe nail."

"Won't the horses come back when they get hungry?" Mattie said.

"The last time my horses ran off, they didn't stop till they reached a ranch twenty-five miles from camp," Walter said. "Took me ten days to find them." He looked at his men. "Who wants to volunteer for a long search?"

"I will," said Jacob. "Norm, fix me a grub pack that'll last several days."

The two men walked back to camp. Mattie noticed they were deep in conversation. Why was Jacob so eager to go find the horses? And what was he talking to Norman about? Before she could speak to Alex and Sophie, Walter said, "Come on, everybody. Let's get busy."

Mattie returned to the wooden table where she had left the cleaning tools. She picked up a brush and began sweeping dirt from Olivia's crevices.

She noticed Sophie hunched over her little dig site. Ellsworth sat nearby. Sophie had made a sunhat for her stuffed elephant from one of Jacob's old socks.

After working a while in the searing sun, Mattie began to feel funny. Not sick, but creepy. Like someone was watching her.

Shielding her eyes, she gazed up into the rocks. On a ledge something flicked out of sight, quick as a lizard. A person? Or the sun playing tricks on her eyes?

Norman fixed the noon meal for the kids and then joined the others at the dig. The team was working longer to make up for being one man short.

Once more, the kids sat under the tree, too hot to eat.

Mattie told the others she was suspicious of Jacob and Norman. Then she mentioned the watcher.

"At first I thought I imagined something moving," she said. "But I *felt* like somebody was staring at me."

"Let's check it out," Alex said. "The men won't miss us."

The kids slipped behind the wagon one

by one. Then they darted to the bottom of the bluff. No one had spotted them.

As they climbed, sharp stones sliced through the soles of their tennis shoes. Mattie fell once, scraping her knee.

"Now I know why Ms. Van Hoven wears hiking boots," she said.

"Watch out for rattlesnakes," Alex warned. "Jacob said their rattles make a sizzling sound. They're really poisonous. If one bites you, you could die."

Goosebumps rose on Mattie's arms. "If I stepped on a snake, I'd die first from a heart attack."

When they reached the top of the rock shelf, they moved slowly between the boulders. Below, they could see their camp and the dig site. But they saw no one or any sign that anyone had been there.

"Maybe you were imagining things," Alex said. "Mom always says you have an overactive imagination."

"That's not true! Besides, I'm doing most of the work on this mission."

"Who's down in a hole all day, shoveling dirt?"

"Hey!" Sophie broke in. "Look what I found."

She held up an apple core. Under the coating of dust, the fruit was beginning to turn brown.

Mattie examined the core. "It hasn't been here too long. It's not that brown. Soph, where did you find this?"

"Over here. By these footprints."

The others followed Sophie to a cone-shaped rock. The ground on the other side was stamped with boot prints. Mattie knelt

and cleared pebbles from one of the prints with a twig.

"The diamond mark!" she said. "Just like on that strange boot print by the horses!"

"Now we know the spy wears these boots," Alex said, "and eats apples."

"Just like Sam," Sophie said, twirling the apple core by its stem.

Mattie smacked her forehead. "How can

we be so dumb? Sam eats apples all the time! He ate one this morning."

"But his boot didn't match the prints we found," said Alex.

"He must own two pairs," Mattie said. "He wore the second pair, the ones with the diamond mark, to let the horses go. Remember when Sam told us about the Bone Wars? He said men sometimes betrayed their leaders. He could be one of those guys! The apple core is evidence."

"But we're not sure," said Alex. "We can't tell Walter until we are."

Sophie handed over Ellsworth's sunhat to wrap up the apple core.

The kids hurried down the bluff and back to the dig site.

"You took a long break," Norman said. "Everything all right?"

Mattie thought fast. "Sophie wasn't feeling well so we kept her out of the heat a while. She's fine now."

"The heat will get to you," Sam agreed. "Alex, I need help with Steggy. She won't let go of this rock. Almost as stubborn as old Walt, here."

Sam was so cheerful, Mattie wondered if she could be wrong about him. After all, it's hardly a crime to have two pairs of boots. Or eat apples.

A shout from the campsite made them all turn. Riding his own horse, Jacob led the other horses, which were tied together in a horse-train. He grinned and waved his hat.

Everyone ran up to him.

"Where were they?" Walter asked, patting his horse's neck.

Jacob dismounted. "At the railroad station. Wandering around as pretty as you please.

Otto said he was going to get word to us later today. He also said our supply shipment will be on the three o'clock train."

"Who wants to pick up the supplies?" Walter asked.

"I will!" Sam offered immediately. "I mean, Jake's just come back. He's tired."

"There isn't that much," Walter told him. "You only need two packhorses."

"I'll let them rest first," said Sam. "Then I'll be off."

Mattie's suspicion returned. She took Alex and Sophie aside.

"Sam's in an awful big hurry to go to the station," she said in a low voice.

Alex nodded. "I wonder if he's going to tell somebody about the allosaurus? Walter said it was valuable, even if it doesn't have a head."

"What about Jacob?" said Sophie.

"He found the horses pretty fast. Maybe he's one of the spies too," Mattie said. "What a mess. At least we have a few days before we have to leave for Laramie."

Purple shadows were falling like curtains when Sam trotted back into camp. The two pack-horses were loaded with more rolls of burlap and sacks of plaster of paris.

Sam went straight to Walter. "Telegram for you." He handed Walter an envelope, then led the horses away.

Walter ripped open the envelope. "Good news. Lavinia Perkins is able to leave Laramie to-morrow morning. She'll be on the noon train. You kids will go back with her in the afternoon."

"Tomorrow!" Alex gasped. "But that's too soon!"

"You will be better off in Laramie," Walter told him.

"We don't want to go to an orphanage," said Mattie. "Please let us stay! We'll work extra hard!"

Sophie looked at Walter with big blue eyes. "Please?"

"Sorry, kids," he said gently. "We're not equipped to take care of children out here. You'll only be in the orphanage long enough to find your folks."

Mattie caught Alex's eye. She knew he was thinking the same thing. They needed more time to prove Sam was a spy.

# — 8 —

# Danger in the Dust

*Clang! Clang!*

A ringing cowbell made Mattie sit up in her bedroll.

"What time is it?" Alex asked, stretching.

"Early," she replied. "Walter must be eager to send us away today."

She hadn't yet come up with a plan to keep them at the dig site. If she didn't hurry, they would be locked in the Laramie orphanage before the day was over.

But when they joined him around the stove, Walter didn't even mention sending them away. He pointed to the sun climbing over the ridge.

"It's going to be hotter than ever today," he said. "We need to get most of our work done before noon."

"How can it possibly be any hotter?" asked Mattie.

Norman banged the coffeepot on the stove. "I'm not cooking today. We're having leftovers for lunch and supper."

After a hasty breakfast of cornbread and coffee, everyone headed for the dig site.

"What time are you leaving for the station?" Sam asked Walter.

Mattie clenched her fists. *You would remind him*, she thought.

"Around ten," Walter replied. "That should give us plenty of time. It'll be hot, but our work here is more important."

"I'll saddle up your horses then," Sam said. He left to tend the horses.

The men hopped into the pit, but Alex hung back. "Sam can't get rid of us fast enough!" he whispered.

"He's on to us," said Mattie.

"We need to do something," Alex said.

"When Daddy wants to catch mice, he sets a trap," Sophie said.

Mattie's face brightened. "That's it! What's the one thing that dinosaur hunters want the most?"

"The head," Sophie stated.

"Yes!" said Mattie. "And what head would Walter like more than anything?"

"Easy," Alex said. "The allosaurus skull."

"What if *we* find the allosaurus skull! Like, over there!" Mattie pointed to the other side of the campsite.

"Why would the skull be way over there?" Alex asked.

"Say it got moved in a flood. Walter said that happened a lot."

"But he also said the skulls were usually crushed," he reminded her.

"We don't *really* find the skull," Mattie said, exasperated. "We just *pretend*."

"We yell and everything and they all come to see. And so will the spy. Gotcha!" He slapped Mattie's and Sophie's palms. "Sounds like a plan!"

"Alex!" Jacob called over to him. "Are you slacking off?"

"I've got to pack," Alex called back.

The kids had little to pack—canteens, their

sunhats. They wore the clothes they'd arrived in. But nobody questioned Alex's excuse.

They took a pick, shovel, and bucket from the pile of equipment and strode to the base of the cliff.

Mattie paced around. "Here's a good spot. Start digging. I'm going back for something." She ran back to camp and returned, lugging a bucket of water and a heavy sack.

"What's that stuff for?" Alex asked.

"The trap."

He swung the pick over his head and into the dirt. Mattie shoveled dirt clods into the bucket. Sophie emptied the bucket away from their "site."

After a while, Mattie said, "The hole is deep enough. Now make a trench around it."

While Alex scraped the dirt, Mattie emptied the sack of white powder into the bucket of water and stirred. Alex helped her pour the white liquid into the trench around the hole.

"Okay," she said, hiding the bucket and empty sack behind a rock. "Let's tell everybody about our big discovery. Remember to talk loud so Sam hears us."

Sophie ran ahead, singing at the top of her lungs, "We found a sku-ull! We found a sku-ull!"

Sam was standing behind the tents with the horses, saddling them up for the journey to Como Station.

Walter and Jacob were wrapping bones in burlap and plaster of paris. They put down their spatulas.

"What did you say?" Walter asked in disbelief.

"It's true!" Mattie said, panting. "We were fooling around by the cliff and we found this *gigantic skull*. It's bigger than a ca—" She started to say *car* but stopped in time.

Norman stared up at them from the bottom of the pit.

"How do you know what a skull looks like?" Norman asked, as he climbed out.

"It's a great big head with eye sockets and sharp pointy teeth." Alex bared his teeth in imitation of a meat-eating dinosaur. "I bet it's part of the allosaurus. The allosaurus's head!" he added loudly. "The *head of the allosaurus!*" He aimed his voice toward the horses.

"We're not deaf," Jacob said.

The men looked at one another. Mattie could tell they were definitely curious. She crossed her fingers and hoped her plan would work.

"Over here!" she said, leading the way.

The others formed a straggly line and

followed her between the tents and around the wagon and horses. Then everyone stopped and gasped.

# Sophie's Discovery

Otto, the stationmaster, stood in the circle of plaster of paris. "Help get me out!" he cried.

Sam came running up. "What's going on here?"

Walter stared at the stationmaster. "Otto, why are you in my camp? And why are you standing in plaster of paris?"

"We caught him in our trap!" Mattie declared. It all made sense now. "Otto is the spy!"

"A spy?" Now Walter stared at the kids.

"Yeah," Mattie said. "Otto has been watching us from the cliff."

"He let the horses go too," Sophie chimed in. She frowned at Otto. "That wasn't very nice."

"Walter, they're just kids," Otto said. "They don't know what they're talking about."

"You still haven't answered my question," Walter said. "Why are you in my camp?"

"He's been here a whole bunch of times," said Mattie. "He knows all about what you've found."

Otto's foot fell back into the trench. "You're not going to listen to them, are you? They don't have any proof."

Mattie crossed her arms. "Oh, yes, we do."

"Pick up your foot," Alex said.

"If I could do that, I'd get out of here!"

"Sam," said Walter. "Help the man."

Sam went over and yanked Otto's right foot out of the hardening plaster. Alex crouched down and peered at the bottom of the sole.

"A diamond mark!" he said. "Just like on the footprints we found."

Walter knelt and looked at the bottom of Otto's upraised boot. "Alex is right. There is a diamond on the heel." He nodded to Sam, who jammed Otto's foot back into the plaster.

"Hey!" Otto cried.

"What's this about footprints?" Walter asked Alex.

"His tracks are all over the place. Where the horses were let loose—"

"Up in the rocks when he watched us," said Sophie.

"We found an apple core too," Mattie added. She remembered the apples on the windowsill of Otto's office. "Otto likes to eat apples."

"So does Sam," said Walter.

"I know," Mattie said sheepishly. "In fact, we thought Sam was the spy until now."

"Thanks a lot," Sam said, but he grinned at her.

Otto waved his arms wildly. "These kids are crazy! Apples, boots. They don't know what they're talking about!"

"We do too!" said Mattie. "He knows every word that comes over the telegraph wire. He knew about the dig because you got messages from Professor Osborn."

Walter frowned. "Telegraph operators are supposed to respect privacy. Better start explaining before I send Jacob for the sheriff."

"I can't talk like this. Get me out first," Otto said.

At Walter's signal, Sam and Norman pulled Otto out. His boots were coated with thick white plaster.

Walter crossed his arm. "You're out. Now talk."

A sheen of sweat coated the bald man's head, and his shoulders sagged in defeat.

"I was promised a stationmaster's job in Dodge City," he began, "but I didn't get it. Instead they stuck me out here in the middle of nowhere. I don't have enough money to quit and I need cash to go back east."

"What does that have to do with our dig?" asked Walter.

"I knew you'd found something important by your messages and the supplies you ordered," Otto admitted. "I figured you'd made an important find."

"So you spied on us," Mattie said.

"What were you planning to do?" Norman wanted to know. "Kill us?"

"Oh, no!" Otto's eyes grew big behind his dusty glasses. "I only wanted to scare you off. I tried to get you to leave."

"Our horses could have been seriously hurt," Walter said angrily. "You still haven't said why you did it."

"To steal fossils," Otto replied. "Not the huge ones, of course. Bones I could put in my saddlebags. Rich private collectors back east will pay a pretty price for real dinosaur bones."

"You're lower than a snake's belly," Jacob said, disgusted. "I'll be glad to go to the sheriff, Walt."

But Walter still had questions. "What made you suspect somebody was hanging around the dig?" he asked the kids.

"Sam told us about poachers and spies in the Bone Wars," answered Mattie. "We were sent—I mean, since we were already here, we thought we'd keep an eye out. Then stuff started to happen."

"You three have certainly earned your keep," said Walter. "I can't thank you enough."

The other men praised Mattie, Alex, and Sophie. Only Mattie saw Otto edge away from the group.

"Hey!" she yelled. "He's getting away!"

In his socks, Otto dashed to the horses and leaped on the back of his horse, which had been tied up just out of sight.

"Mount up!" Jacob shouted. "Catch him!"

But Walter held up a hand. "He can't go far barefooted. If he goes back to the station, he'll be arrested. After we file our report, Otto won't be able to set foot on a Union Pacific train from Omaha to Sacramento. We have other things to do."

They walked back toward camp. Suddenly Sophie ran ahead. She hopped around her private dig site.

"I knew it was here!" she cried, jumping up and down.

"What is she talking about?" Alex asked Mattie.

"That's the little dig she's been working on," she replied. "I let her borrow a brush and cleaning tool. She was just messing around."

Walter reached Sophie's dig and knelt down. His hand swept away loose sand and then he gave a low whistle.

"If Sophie was just messing around," he said, "I want her to work for me!"

Everyone stood around Sophie's dig. An entire skeleton, no more than ten inches long, was preserved in stone. From its tiny claws to the tip of its tail, the skeleton was perfect.

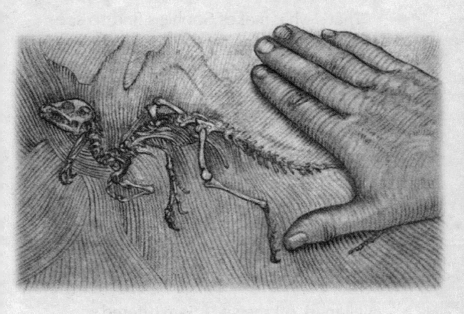

"What is it?" Mattie asked.

"Looks like a lizard to me," said Alex. "Or a bird. But its wings are missing."

"It's not a lizard or a bird," Walter told them. "It's the best thing of all—a baby dinosaur!"

"What's so great about a baby dinosaur?"

Mattie wanted to know. "It's not big like the dinosaurs you found."

"That's what makes Sophie's find so special," Jacob said. "Baby dinosaurs didn't have much of a chance in the world. They often got eaten. We rarely find one, and we've *never* found one as fine as this."

"Best of all," Walter added, "the skull is intact!" He picked up Sophie and twirled her around. "Thank you, Sophie! Professor Osborn will be delighted to receive this little guy for his museum."

"I'll mark off the site," Sam offered.

"You know, we could use some extra help out here," said Jacob. "Why don't you ask Professor Osborn for another field assistant?"

"I will," said Walter.

Jacob took his pocket watch from his pocket. "Walt, that train will be at the station in thirty minutes."

Walter was still admiring the baby dinosaur. "We can make it if we hurry. Otto won't be there to bring the train in. It won't stop if no one is on the platform."

"I'll saddle the horses," Jacob offered.

"I'll fill your canteens," said Norman.

In the rush, Mattie, Alex, and Sophie were forgotten.

"Time to leave," Mattie whispered. "We did what we came here to do."

"I wish we could stay," Alex said wistfully.

Mattie nodded. "Being a paleontologist is hard work. But it makes you feel good to make discoveries." Then she added, "I won't miss the food!"

Alex extended the spyglass. Mattie took one end. Sophie started to reach for the other end, but dropped Ellsworth.

"Hurry!" Mattie urged. "Before they see us!"

Sophie picked up her stuffed animal. Mattie barely noticed her slip something else into her pocket. Finally Sophie touched the other end of the spyglass.

Mattie closed her eyes. She still didn't like this part, falling through the black tunnel sparked with colored lights, but she was getting used to it.

*Scritch-scratch*! Her tennis shoes sounded like sandpaper on the floor of the tower room. Alex and Sophie appeared next. Their faces were streaked with dirt.

"Good grief!" Mattie said. "We'd better clean up before Mom sees us."

"I'll get the letter," Alex said. "We can read it in my room after."

He crunched over to the desk and opened the top drawer. He put the spyglass inside its velvet box and tucked it back into the secret compartment. Then he opened the cubbyhole's false back and took out a letter.

"Is it from Ms. Van Hoven?" Mattie asked.

Alex nodded. "I wonder what she'll tell us about this trip. Seems like we already know everything!"

"I learned a lot," said Mattie. She glanced back at the desk and hoped the next Travel Guide would come soon.

They started for the bookcase door.

"Come on, Soph," Alex said.

"Wait a minute." Sophie ran over to the desk and opened the middle drawer. She took something very small out of her pocket and laid it inside. A tiny, perfect dinosaur tooth gleamed in the morning light.

"Till next time," Sophie whispered, then closed the drawer gently.

Dear Mattie, Alex, and Sophie:

Did you like being on a dinosaur dig in 1898? If you went on a fossil hunt today, the food would be better, Mattie! But one thing that hasn't changed is the hard work.

You found out a lot about early paleontology from Walter Granger and his field workers. But yes, Alex, there is more to learn. There always is!

Dr. Caspar Wistar found the first dinosaur fossil in America. He unearthed a thighbone in New Jersey in 1787. In 1800 dinosaur tracks were discovered on a farm in Massachusetts.

In 1838 workers digging on a farm in Haddonfield, New Jersey, stumbled on very large bones. It was the first nearly complete dinosaur skeleton.

Twenty years later, scientist Joseph Leidy studied the bones and named the dinosaur hadrosaurus. Professor Leidy is often called "the father of American paleontology."

Edward Cope and O. C. Marsh were two young scientists who knew Professor Leidy and were friends. Once, Cope showed Marsh the skeleton of a fossil of a new dinosaur. Marsh said the backbones were facing the wrong way. Professor Leidy was asked to decide who was right. Leidy took the dinosaur's head and put it on the tail! Marsh had been right. Cope was mad at Marsh.

From then on the two friends became enemies. When dinosaur bones were discovered in the western states, Cope and Marsh tried to see who could find the most new dinosaur species. Teams of fossil hunters combed Colorado, Nebraska, and Wyoming. The race became ugly. Cope and Marsh used spies and stole workers from each other. Cope even stole a trainload of fossils from Marsh. In the end, Marsh won the Bone Wars by discovering and naming eighty-six new dinosaurs, including the allosaurus. Cope only found fifty-six.

Walter Granger was born in Middletown Springs, Vermont, in 1872. As a boy, he rambled over the mountains. He watched animals and studied nature. When he was seventeen, Walter was offered a job at the American Museum of Natural History in New York City. At the museum Walter became interested in fossils. In 1898 he traveled west and discovered Bone Cabin Quarry.

Bone Cabin Quarry turned out to be one of the greatest dinosaur digs in North America. Walter and his men found an allosaurus, a brontosaurus, a stegosaurus, and other dinosaurs. For the next five years, their fossils filled railroad cars—sixty-four dinosaurs, five turtles, and four crocodiles.

Later, Walter went to Egypt, Mongolia, and China to look for fossils. He helped discover Peking man. Fossils of this early man were 300,000 to 500,000 years old!

Walter Granger died in 1941. He, and other early fossil hunters, opened the way for today's paleontologists. They worked in searing heat and dangerous storms. They were bitten by snakes and insects. But they never gave up.

Remember how Walter Granger made copies of dinosaur tracks? Spies can use that trick too. While you wait for the next Travel Guide, I'm leaving you instructions to practice making plaster prints.

Where are you going next? I'm not supposed to do this, but here's a little hint: think green.

Yours in time,
"Ms. Van Hoven"

# TIME SPIES MISSION NO. 2
# MAKE PLASTER CASTS OF TRACKS

Spies sometimes collect human tracks—footprints. They can identify the person who left the footprint by making a cast.

Remember when Mattie spotted the diamond-shaped mark on the strange footprint? You could have made a plaster cast of the footprint. Then you could have compared the cast to Otto's boot.

Until your next adventure, your mission is to learn how to make plaster casts. Good luck!

# WHAT YOU NEED:

Plaster of paris
Strips of cardboard about 3 inches wide
Large plastic cup
Plastic spoon
Petroleum jelly or vegetable shortening
Paper clips
Bottle of water

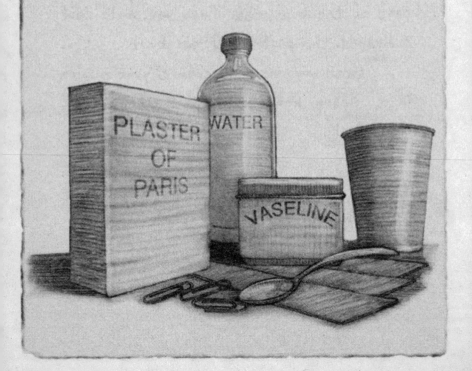

## WHAT YOU DO:

1.  Find an animal or human track.
2.  Mix plaster of paris with water in the cup. Mixture should be thick, like cream.
3.  Form a ring with a cardboard strip to fit around the track. Fasten with paper clip.
4.  Grease inside of ring with petroleum jelly or vegetable shortening.
5.  Place ring around track so track is inside circle.
6.  Pour mixture over track. Do not fill ring to the top.
7.  Let set for an hour or until plaster is hard.
8.  Remove ring.

# TIME SPIES

When Mr. and Mrs. Chapman move their family
to rural Virginia to run the Gray Horse Inn,
Mattie, Alex, and Sophie Chapman are sure it
will be the most boring summer of their lives.
But as soon as they discover a hidden spyglass,
the three kids find more adventure than they
could ever imagine!

## Secret in the Tower
### September 2006

## Bones in the Badlands
### October 2006

For more information visit www.mirrorstonebooks.com
for ages six to ten